The Mask of Power

Spyro

versus

the Mega Monsters

by Onk Beakman

Grosset & Dunlap

An Imprint of Penguin Group (USA) Inc.

GROSSET & DUNLAP
Published by the Penguin Group
Penguin Group (USA) Inc., 375 Hudson Street, New York, New York 10014, USA
Penguin Group (Canada), 90 Eglinton Avenue East, Suite 700, Toronto, Ontario
M4P 2Y3, Canada (a division of Pearson Penguin Canada Inc.)
Penguin Books Ltd, 80 Strand, London WC2R 0RL, England
Penguin Ireland, 25 St Stephen's Green, Dublin 2, Ireland
(a division of Penguin Books Ltd)
Penguin Group (Australia), 707 Collins Street, Melbourne, Victoria 3008,
Australia (a division of Pearson Australia Group Pty Ltd)
Penguin Books India Pvt Ltd, 11 Community Centre,
Panchsheel Park, New Delhi—110 017, India
Penguin Group (NZ), 67 Apollo Drive, Rosedale, Auckland 0632, New Zealand
(a division of Pearson New Zealand Ltd)
Penguin Books, Rosebank Office Park, 181 Jan Smuts Avenue,
Parktown North 2193, South Africa
Penguin China, B7 Jaiming Center, 27 East Third Ring Road North,
Chaoyang District, Beijing 100020, China

Penguin Books Ltd, Registered Offices: 80 Strand, London WC2R 0RL, England

Written by Cavan Scott
Illustrated by Tino Santanach

© 2012 Activision Publishing, Inc. Skylanders Universe is a trademark and
Spyro and Activision are registered trademarks of Activision Publishing, Inc.
Published by Grosset & Dunlap, a division of Penguin Young Readers Group,
345 Hudson Street, New York, New York 10014. GROSSET & DUNLAP is a
trademark of Penguin Group (USA) Inc.
Printed in the U.S.A.

ISBN 978-0-448-46355-1   10 9 8 7 6 5 4 3 2 1

About the Author

Onk Beakman knew he wanted to be a world-famous author from the moment he was hatched. In fact, the book-loving penguin was so keen that he wrote his first novel while still inside his egg (to this day, nobody is entirely sure where he got the tiny pencil and notebook from).

Growing up on the icy wastes of Skylands's Frozen Desert was difficult for a penguin who hated the cold. While his brothers plunged into the freezing waters, Onk could be found with his beak buried in a book and a pen clutched in his flippers.

Yet his life changed forever when a giant floating head appeared in the skies above the tundra. It was Kaos, attempting to melt the icecaps so he could get his grubby little hands on an ancient weapon buried beneath the snow.

Onk watched open-beaked as Spyro swept in and sent the evil Portal Master packing. From that day on, Onk knew that he must chronicle the Skylanders' greatest adventures. He traveled the length and breadth of Skylands, collecting every tale he could find about Master Eon's brave champions.

Today, Onk writes from a shack on the beautiful sands of Blistering Beach, where he lives with his two pet sea cucumbers.

Chapter One

THE STINKY SWAMP

Skylands is the most amazing place in the universe. Nothing compares to it. Nothing at all. It is made up of thousands . . . no, millions . . . no, gazillions of floating islands. Each one is totally different from the next, but all are full of adventure. Magic courses through every rock, plant, and animal—even the sheep. Dragons swoop through the sky, dirt sharks burrow deep beneath the ground, and nothing is what it seems. Some of the islands are beautiful. Some of the islands are terrifying. Yet all of them are special . . . even the smelly ones.

Take the Stinky Swamp, for example. The name is a bit of a giveaway. The place positively reeks. In fact, it's the second smelliest place in all of Skylands. The first, in case you were wondering, is Kaos's sock drawer. Kaos is an evil Portal Master extraordinaire, dark wizard and all-around bad guy (prepare yourself—you'll meet him later). Imagine the aroma of rancid cabbage mixed with wet dog hair and a skunk's old bedsheets. Revolting, eh? Well, multiply that by ten and you'll get an idea of the potency of Kaos's foul-smelling footwear. Disgusting.

The Stinky Swamp smells better, but just barely. The entire island is smothered in funky marshes, rotting trees, and fetid fruit. And that's not the worst part. If the smell doesn't get you, the vegetation will.

Vampire vines hang from every branch, ready to snake around unsuspecting passersby, while Chompy Pods cluster around the roots of every twisted tree.

In case you don't know, Chompy Pods are plants that spore Chompies—small green beasties with ferocious appetites. Chompies are basically mouths on legs. Mouths bristling with razor-sharp teeth. Mouths that are best avoided.

One way or another, the Stinky Swamp is not a nice place to be. Which is why it is surprising that people go there at all. But they do. Not in great numbers, obviously, but enough to get the island listed in the official *1001 Places to Visit in Skylands* guidebook ten years in a row.

Why?

Well, the reason folks repeatedly risk life, limb, and their nasal passages is that the Stinky Swamp boasts the tastiest fish in all of Skylands. They are completely and utterly delicious.

One fisherman, a humble Mabu by the name of Nort, had been coming here for years, enduring the smells and avoiding the wildlife. Every morning he'd travel to the swamp by hot air balloon, untie the boat he kept moored near the edge of the marsh, and pop a clothespin on his nose. Then he would push off into the middle of the bayou, cast off, and sit back, waiting for the fish to bite.

Nort had been coming here for so long, he'd even started to get used to the stench. He liked it here. You hardly saw anyone, and as long as you were careful—and didn't breathe too deeply—you were safe.

Usually.

But not today. Today that all changed.

Today, Nort was drifting through the marshland, dozing in his boat, waking only to bat away the flies that buzzed around his head.

This is the life, Nort thought. *Just me, my rod, and miles of rank water. Heaven.*

But Nort wasn't alone. Something else was in the swamp with him. Something big.

Nort awoke with a start as a sound reverberated around the bayou. It was like nothing he'd ever heard. A deep, rumbling roar. He pushed his hat back from his eyes and looked around nervously. Where had it come from? He strained his ears but could only hear the usual sounds of the swamp— the chirp of the insects and the occasional shriek of birds high in the canopy.

ROAR!

There it was again, a growl so loud it rattled the oars of his boat. Nort swallowed.

Perhaps he'd had enough fishing. Perhaps he'd call it a day. Perhaps he'd head home before he came face-to-face with whatever had made that petrifying sound.

It was too late. From the corner

of his eye, Nort saw something huge fling itself from the undergrowth and soar through the air. He spun around just in time to see it crash into the water, sending huge ripples rushing toward his boat. He hung on as the small craft was tossed this way and that, and watched in dismay as one of his oars slipped into the water.

All became calm again, and Nort could feel his heart slamming against his chest. Shaking with fear, he peered over the side of the boat and found himself staring straight into a pair of huge, wide eyes.

Nort screamed in panic and grabbed his one remaining oar to defend himself. Not that it did him any good. The monster thrust its head from beneath the water and sent boat, fishing equipment, and Mabu flying high into the air. Just when Nort thought the day couldn't get any worse, a massive slobbering tongue shot up from the creature's mouth and grabbed him. Before he could utter another yelp, Nort was pulled down into the monster's mouth. With a satisfied croak, the creature disappeared back under the water.

Nort's little boat landed on the water with a splash and drifted silently down the river.

Chapter Two

THE DAYBRINGER FLAME

The Goliath Drow loomed over Drill Sergeant. Before Spyro the Dragon could warn his friend, the Arkeyan bulldozer was knocked aside by a swipe of one of the dark elf's massive spiked shields. Drill Sergeant skidded along the ground, his auto-blaster spinning helplessly, and slammed straight into Trigger Happy.

The golden gunslinger yelped as Drill Sergeant rolled over him, his pistols tumbling from his red furry hands. "Get him off me," he shrieked, even as Drill

Sergeant tried to right himself. "Get him off me!"

Behind them, the Drow raised its shields, an arrogant leer spreading across its flat features. The two Skylanders were seconds from being pummeled into the ground. The fight was not going well.

"What are you waiting for, old boy?"

Beside Spyro, Jet-Vac was desperately trying to prime his vacuum gun to help his friends. "You need to do something."

Spyro knew the Sky Baron was right. This was it. The moment of truth.

Spyro took in a deep breath, feeling the fire ignite in his belly. He closed his eyes for a second, remembering the advice Master

Eon had given him: *Focus the flame, Spyro. Mold it. Command it.*

The fire swelled deep inside him, burning hot, ready to escape. He could hear Drill Sergeant calling his name, desperate for him to do something, anything.

Focus the flame.

Spyro opened his eyes. The Drow was charging toward him, its twin shields held high. Spyro opened his mouth and breathed a blazing ball of dragon fire straight at the advancing Drow.

At least that was the idea. Instead of a giant ball of fire, a column of white-hot flame burst from Spyro's open mouth with such force that the

little purple dragon was blown right off his feet. He rocketed backward, slamming into a tree behind him and crashing to the ground, stunned. He lay there for a second, ears ringing, not wanting to open his eyes again, not wanting to see what damage he had caused this time.

"Beep-be-be-beep. That wasn't supposed to happen, was it, sir?" came a harsh, mechanical voice.

"No," replied another. A deep, resonant voice. Master Eon's voice. "No, it wasn't."

Spyro winced. Not again. Sheepishly, he opened one eye. The Drow stood in front of him, completely unscathed, grinning from ear to ear. The same could not be said for the grounds of Eon's citadel. The usually lush grass was scorched and the cabbage patch was ablaze. Poor old Drill Sergeant was still on his side, the blistered red paint on his metalwork covered in soot, and Trigg's usually orange fur was blackened from head to foot. Spyro's head dropped as Master Eon stepped from behind the triumphant dark elf. Even the Portal Master's snow-white beard was looking decidedly singed. Eon waved his hand and the Goliath Drow vanished in a puff of smoke. It had been

an illusion, just part of Spyro's training session. Spyro's *failed* training session.

Spyro frowned. "I'm sorry," he mumbled, but Eon cut off the apology with a raised hand.

"There is no need to apologize, Spyro," Eon said, clicking his fingers. To his right, Drill Sergeant tipped back on his tracks as if by magic. Which is exactly what it was. "These things take time."

"Not for me," Spyro muttered under his breath. He wasn't used to this. He was a Skylander, a champion personally selected by Eon to protect Skylands from the forces of Darkness. Each Skylander had unique powers and abilities, but Eon never let them rest on their laurels. Spyro could understand why. Skylands was just too important. From here, you could travel to any location in the universe. It was a stepping stone to all of creation. If evil ever conquered Skylands, it could spread unchecked to every world in existence. So Eon trained them hard, teaching them new ways to fight. New ways to defend.

Usually Spyro was a quick learner. Usually he mastered new abilities in a matter of hours. Why was this difficult? He'd been practicing the Daybringer Flame for days. It was supposed to generate a ball of fire so big and bright that it lit up the sky. Instead, Spyro kept producing wild, uncontrollable flames that burned everything to a crisp. Eon had created plenty of targets: images of trolls, cyclopses, Drow—even Kaos, the evil Portal Master who had vowed to take over Skylands. But it was hopeless. Why couldn't Spyro get it right?

"Spyro, you're being awfully hard on yourself." Jet-Vac had slung his vacuum-blaster over his shoulder, his role in the

training session at an end. "You can't be good at everything."

"Yes I can," Spyro snapped back, before biting his tongue. Getting angry with his friends wasn't helping. He set his jaw and looked up at his master, eyes sparkling with determination. "Let's try again."

Behind them, Drill Sergeant let out a whimper of dismay, although Trigger Happy was already on his feet, giggling happily to himself. Bizarrely, the gun-loving gremlin seemed to be enjoying being continually frazzled.

Eon smiled warmly, resting on his staff. "I think we could all do with a break. Let's continue our training tomorrow."

Spyro tried to ignore the sigh of relief that came from Drill Sergeant's general direction. This was completely humiliating. Not wanting to meet his friend's eyes, Spyro glanced up at the Core of Light, the towering beacon that kept Darkness at bay. How could he defend the Core when he couldn't master something as simple as the Daybringer Flame?

Perhaps Eon was right. Perhaps he just needed to take his mind off his training. Perhaps he was trying *too* hard.

He turned back to Eon, but the Portal Master was no longer smiling. Instead, the old man was standing with his eyes closed, a look of concern etched onto his face.

"Master? Are you all right?"

Eon reached up and massaged his temple, as if trying to banish a sudden headache. "Something is wrong."

Spyro felt his spines bristle.

"It's Stealth Elf. She is calling for a Portal. Come."

Without another word, Eon turned on his heel and marched toward the citadel. Spyro exchanged a worried look with Jet-

Vac and ran after the Portal Master.

The Portal of Power hummed to life as soon as Eon entered the chamber. These ancient artifacts were found scattered across Skylands. No one knew who originally created them, but only Portal Masters like Eon—and Kaos—could use them. Once activated, they could transport you anywhere in the universe. Some even believed they could send you back in time.

Eon's Portal was the biggest Spyro had ever seen, carved with a myriad of magical symbols. As Eon strode nearer, the stone top of the Portal began to glow, the indigo light  intensifying with every step. Spyro felt his scales tingle as the atmosphere in the majestic chamber changed. It was as if the very air was buzzing with excitement.

Suddenly, a door to their left was thrown open and a small figure bustled into the Portal Chamber. It was Hugo, Master Eon's right-hand Mabu. Hugo had been Eon's assistant for as long as anyone could remember. The citadel probably couldn't function without him. He was the chief librarian, record keeper, and guardian of the ancient scrolls, and he always did the washing up. No wonder he always looked flustered.

"Master Eon, thank heavens," he started, rushing up to the Portal Master on his tiny legs. "I bring grave news."

Eon didn't even look in Hugo's direction. He continued striding forward, his staff tapping against the stone slabs. "Not now, Hugo."

"But Master, it's awfully important—"

"As is this." Eon had reached the side of the Portal, which was now burning with such brilliance that Spyro was forced to screw up his eyes. The Portal Master raised his arms and commanded the Portal to open. Immediately a column of light shot up from its surface to the vaulted ceiling high above. With the sound of the universe ripping apart and instantly reforming, a figure appeared in the light, leaped forward, and rolled gracefully along

the floor, finishing in a crouch. As Eon closed the Portal, the newcomer got to her feet and turned to her master.

"Stealth Elf," Eon said, approaching the female Skylander. "What is wrong?"

The elf flicked her long blue ponytail over a shoulder and looked at Eon with concerned eyes.

"It's a monster, Master," she replied, her voice soft but steely. "A terrible monster."

Chapter Three

CHOMPY ATTACK

The smell hit Spyro as soon as he flew out of the Portal. He knew that the Stinky Swamp had been given its name for a reason, but this was ridiculous. Almost immediately his eyes began to water at the reek.

Stealth Elf appeared behind him, dragonfang daggers drawn and ready for action. She didn't seem fazed by the smell, but then again she had been patrolling the acrid area for most of the morning. The elf's glowing eyes darted around the clearing and, once she was convinced there was no immediate danger, visibly relaxed.

"This way," she said, disappearing through the bushes in front of them. Spyro followed, being careful to avoid a Vampire vine that was snaking around an old rotting tree. He didn't want to get tangled in that.

He found Stealth Elf crouched beside the riverside, looking down at the foul-smelling mud. "Here it is," she whispered.

Spyro looked over her shoulder and his eyes widened. Stealth Elf had been right. There, in the soft, squelchy mud was a massive webbed footprint. It was so big

Spyro could have easily curled up in it.

"They're all over the water's edge," Stealth Elf explained, her large pointed ears twitching as she listened for sounds of danger. "Dozens of them."

"Do you think it's a water dragon?" Spyro asked, comparing the size of the print with his own paw. His looked worryingly small in comparison.

"If it is, it's the biggest I've ever—"

Stealth Elf's words were cut off by the sound of a scream.

"Someone's in trouble," shouted Spyro. "Come on!"

"Help me," the voice squealed as Spyro burst into the clearing. "Please. Somebody help!"

It was a Mabu, running around and around in circles, one hand keeping a battered hat on his head and the other

swatting away the three Chompies
that were snapping at his legs.

When he spotted the two Skylanders,
his face beamed with delight.

"Skylanders! Thank heaven, I . . . ow!"

The delight faded in an instant as one
of the Chompies sunk its long teeth into
the Mabu's plump posterior.

"Ow! Ow! Ow! Ow! Ow!"

The Mabu charged this way and that, trying—and failing—to shake the backside-biter from his bottom.

"Get it off me! Get it off me!"

Stealth Elf sprinted forward. The two remaining Chompies spun in her direction, fangs flashing hungrily in the dull light. They raced toward her, but she changed direction at the last minute and shot off to the side. The Chompies couldn't stop in time and crashed into each other. They fell back, stunned, but weren't down for long. The snapping critters got back to their feet and whizzed around. Their beady eyes stretched wide with surprise.

Where there had been one Stealth Elf, there now stood two. Delight flickered over the Chompies' faces. More legs to chew! Fantastic! They scuttled forward, launched themselves into the air, and threw their jaws open, ready to bite down. But when their mouths snapped shut, their teeth closed on empty air and they crashed through both Stealth Elves as if they weren't there. Which they weren't.

Spyro grinned as the Chompies bounced like bewildered beach balls across the clearing. Of course, they didn't know that Stealth Elf could create decoy doubles of herself to confuse her enemies. In a blur of motion, the real Stealth Elf appeared behind them and, with a swift kick, sent them both flying into a nearby tree.

Two down, one to go.

Spyro turned back to the Mabu, who was still racing around the clearing, the Chompy fixed firmly to his rear.

"Stand still!" Spyro shouted out.

The Mabu was so shocked he skidded to a halt, his eyes widening as he saw Spyro lower his head.

"But, but, but . . ." the Mabu stuttered. "Exactly," yelled Spyro, breaking into a run. "Sprint charge!"

The Chompy let out a little squeak as Spyro's horns butted into its side. With a flick of his head, Spyro sent the creature spinning through the air, a scrap of the Mabu's stripy underwear still clenched between its teeth. It crashed through the branches and sailed out of sight.

"That's the last we'll see of them," Stealth Elf

said, slipping her daggers back into her belt.

"Good thing, too," agreed Spyro. "We need to get to the bottom of the footprint mystery."

"Can we not mention bottoms?" moaned the Mabu, rubbing his sore behind.

Chapter Four

THE SWAMP MONSTER

Spyro waited patiently as Snuckles, the Mabu they had rescued from the Chompies, tied his hat to his backside. It only just covered the ragged hole in his pants, and the corks jangled every time he moved. Still, it was the best they could do for now.

"I still don't get why you're here," Spyro said when Snuckles had finished his emergency repairs. "You don't look like you've come to fish. You haven't even got a rod."

"Oh no, I hate fish," admitted Snuckles. "They make me break out in a nasty rash. It was my best friend who was the fisherman."

"Your friend?" asked Stealth Elf.

"Yes," replied Snuckles. "Nort came here two days ago and never returned. I've been worried sick."

"So you came here looking for him?"

Snuckles nodded, his bottom lip quivering. "But if there's some kind of swamp monster—"

"We don't know that for sure," cut in Spyro. A sniveling Mabu was the last thing they wanted—and this fellow seemed to snivel at the drop of a hat. "We'll help you find him."

"You will?" Snuckles brightened immediately.

"We will?" Stealth Elf crossed her arms. "Before or after we've tracked down the owner of the giant webbed feet?"

Spyro sighed. Stealth Elf may have been a highly trained ninja, able to sneak up silently on anyone, but sometimes she had the tact of a rampaging Cyclops Mammoth. He opened his mouth, but before he could retort, a loud belching noise boomed through the air.

"How rude," sniffed Snuckles, putting his hands on his hips in disgust. "Didn't your mother tell you not to burp in public?"

"That wasn't me," Spyro hissed, the spines flattening against his head.

Another deafening croak thundered around the clearing.

"But if it wasn't you . . ." started Stealth Elf, but she didn't get a chance to finish her sentence. Without warning, something long, pink, and slimy shot out of the bushes. It slammed into Stealth Elf's back and stuck firm. She twisted, trying to see what had attached itself to her, but was pulled off her feet as the muscular tentacle whipped back into the undergrowth, dragging Stealth Elf with it.

"What was that?" screamed a terrified Snuckles, but Spyro didn't answer. Instead he leaped after her, crashing through branches and brambles until he smashed through to the other side.

His mouth dropped open as he skidded to a halt, not quite believing what he saw. There, in his path, sat an orange toad. Yet this was no ordinary orange toad. It was an orange toad the size of a very large and very fat elephant. It also looked far from happy.

Horrible noises were emanating from its oversize belly, and its eyes boggled and bulged. Suddenly, without warning, it let out an almighty belch and spewed something onto the ground in front of Spyro. Not something. Somebody. It was Stealth Elf, covered in slimy toad spit.

"What happened?" Spyro asked, looking her up and down.

"It disagreed with something it ate," she replied, pushing slime-encrusted hair from her eyes. "Me!"

Snuckles stumbled through the plants and scrambled to a halt.

"No!" Spyro shouted. "Stay out of the way, Snuckles."

"But, but, but . . ." stammered Snuckles, "that's a . . . a . . . a . . ."

"Massive toad with warts the size of your head. I know." In front of them, the toad was rearing up on its back legs, obviously ready to attack. "Stealth, get Snuckles out of here. I'll deal with this."

Perhaps this is just the time to practice my Daybringer Flame after all, he said to himself. But Stealth Elf wasn't herding Snuckles out of danger. She was swaying on her feet and turning an unhealthy shade of green, which was quite an achievement for an elf.

"I don't feel too good," she slurred, tottering forward, "Sleepy. So . . . sleepy."

Her knees buckled beneath her and Stealth Elf fell against Spyro. Spyro grabbed for his friend and helped her slip gently to the floor. She was snoring peacefully by the time her head hit the ground.

"That's it!" Spyro exclaimed, looking back up at the toad.

"What's it?" asked Snuckles, too terrified to move, save for his knees, which knocked together.

"I've got a photographic memory," Spyro explained. "I never forget anything, and I've seen one of those before."

"Where?"

"All over the place. They're really common."

Snuckles wrung his hands together.

"It doesn't look that common to me. It looks furious."

"But that's just it," Spyro continued, looking at the bright blue markings that covered the creature's broad back. "It's a titchy toad. You can usually fit three of them in the palm of your hand, they're so small."

"You'd have to have pretty big hands."

"Exactly. So what on earth has made it grow so—"

Spyro yawned.

The dragon shook his head, trying to clear it. Spyro had never felt so tired. It was almost as if his legs could no longer carry his weight. He looked down at them, willing them to stop shaking. Of course! The titchy toad had highly toxic spittle that it used to

send its victims to sleep. Stealth Elf had been covered in the stuff. When he'd helped her to the ground, the toad spit had smeared all over his scales. He was falling asleep, too.

"Spyro, wake up!"

He could hear Snuckles screaming, but it was all he could do to stay awake. His eyelids felt like lead weights. Surely no one would mind if he took a little nap?

"Help me!"

What? Spyro forced his eyes open and gazed sleepily back. Odd. Why was Snuckles scrabbling around on the ground? And why was he moving backward?

"It's got my ankle!" the Mabu shrieked.

"It's pulling me back."

Sure enough, a Vampire vine had wrapped itself around Snuckles's struggling ankle and was dragging him into the undergrowth.

Snuckles reached out toward the exhausted dragon, but grabbed on to more than he bargained for. With an earsplitting croak, the toad shot out its tongue, slamming it between Snuckles's outstretched arms. It stuck fast and the hapless Mabu suddenly found himself caught in the middle of a titanic tug-of-war. The vine continued to try to pull him back into the woodland while the tongue tried to yank him forward into the toad's waiting mouth. If Spyro didn't act soon, the poor Mabu would be torn in two.

He tried to move, but the effort of lifting just one wing was too great. Then a huge, webbed foot crashed down on Spyro's back,

pinning him to the muddy
ground. In order to get more
purchase, the toad had stepped
right on top of the sleepy Skylander.

Can today get any worse? thought
Spyro as a flash of blinding light burst all
over the clearing. Spots danced in front
of Spyro's tired eyes, but when his vision
cleared he realized that yes, today could get
much, much worse.

There, in the center of the clearing, stood Kaos himself.

Chapter Five

AN UNLIKELY ALLY

"Well, well," crowed Kaos, brandishing a large scarlet staff. "Look what we have here. Two snoozy Skylanders sleeping on the job."

Spyro tried to snarl, but even that was too much effort. It was all he could do to stay awake.

"Er, Master?" said another voice. It was Glumshanks, Kaos's loyal sidekick. When Kaos had first attempted to take over Skylands, Glumshanks had been by his side, and there the troll had remained through every fiendish plan and crushing defeat that followed.

Today, the long-suffering servant was standing with a large pair of shears in his spindly hands. "Master?" he repeated, "Shouldn't we do something about *that?*" He nodded his head toward the gigantic amphibian that was still trying to pull Snuckles into its gaping maw.

"Wah!" cried Kaos, jumping slightly at his butler's voice. "How many times have I told you not to sneak up on me? Well, what are you waiting for, FOOL? We need to do something about *that.*" The evil Portal Master jabbed the pointy red ruby at the end of his staff toward the toad.

"Of course, Master," muttered Glumshanks. "How silly of me to forget."

"Sometimes I don't know why I bother." Kaos shrugged, shaking his head at Spyro as if he was apologizing for his henchman's inadequacies, before turning his attention back to Glumshanks. "You get pruning. I'll deal with this monstrosity."

Spyro couldn't work out what was happening. When Kaos had appeared, he'd assumed this had all been a trap. Kaos had two main ambitions. First and foremost, he wanted to destroy the Core of Light so Darkness could cover Skylands. Secondly (and largely so he could achieve the first) he longed to defeat the Skylanders once and for all. He never succeeded, of course, but the one thing you could say about Kaos was that he was persistent.

Of course, you could also say he had dreadful personal hygiene, atrocious fashion sense, and the kind of face not even his own mother could love, but now wasn't the time.

Surely this was Kaos's idea of a dream come true. Two Skylanders incapacitated and completely at his mercy. Spyro wouldn't stand a chance if Kaos attacked now. So why was the Portal Master pointing his staff, not at Spyro or Stealth Elf, but at the giant toad?

For that matter, why was Glumshanks setting about the vines that were coiled around Snuckles's ankle? The lanky troll was attacking the snaking creepers like a demon gardener, all flashing blades and snipping shears. Perhaps Spyro was dreaming? Yes, that had to be it.

With a final "snip," Glumshanks hacked through the vine. The malicious plant thrashed around wildly as Snuckles was released from its grip. The Mabu shot through the air toward the toad, the massive pink tongue contracting as if it were elastic. Snuckles smacked into the amphibian's nose, stunning the creature.

"Ooooh," mocked Kaos. "That's gotta hurt. Right between the eyes." As he spoke, dark red lightning crackled around the gem mounted at the end of the staff. "Now, listen up, you amphibian abomination— I, Kaos, will introduce you to your UNIMAGINABLE DOOM!"

A bolt of deep crimson energy burst from the end of Kaos's staff and slammed into the toad. The creature croaked in surprise and, in a puff of pinkish smoke, vanished from sight.

"Ha!" Kaos punched the air in triumph. "I am unstoppable!" He spun around to face Snuckles, obviously expecting adoration, cheers, or at least a little polite applause. The shaking Mabu didn't applaud. In fact, he started to cry. Kaos's face fell.

"Is that it?" the Portal Master exclaimed. "No thanks? No praise? I don't know if you noticed, but I just saved your life!!"

Yes, Spyro thought, *and I still don't know why*. This wasn't Kaos's style at all. "He's upset," Spyro explained. "The danger may have passed, but his best friend is still missing."

"Nort!" Snuckles wailed, sitting back on his hat. "He must have been eaten by that . . . by that . . . thing." The Mabu dissolved into more sobs.

"Oh, him," Kaos said, as if he'd just remembered something. "Why didn't you say? I rescued him hours ago."

Kaos clapped his hands and a Portal opened, depositing another shocked-looking Mabu into the mud.

"Nort?" Snuckles asked, not quite believing his eyes. "Nort, is that you?"

The newcomer blinked, recognition spreading across his face.

"Snuckles! I never thought I'd see you again!"

The two Mabu hugged.

"You're Nort?" Spyro asked. "Snuckles's friend?" Nort nodded happily. "And Kaos had you all this time? What did he do to you?"

"Do?" Nort asked. "I'll tell you what he did. I was about to be eaten alive by a gigantic toad when he rescued me. He took me back to his lair . . ."

"Er, I call it Kaos Towers now," Kaos interjected. "Lair just sounds a bit too . . . evil."

Spyro's brows raised. Since when did Kaos worry about sounding evil?

"This man is a hero!" Nort insisted.

"He certainly is!" agreed Snuckles, beaming wildly. "Three cheers for Kaos! Hip hip—"

"Oh, stop it." Kaos blushed, before adding slyly, "Then again, if you must . . ."

Spyro watched slack-jawed as the two Mabu cheered their savior—the most wicked man Skylands had ever known. It was a good thing Stealth Elf was asleep. She would never believe this.

"Hip hip!"

"Hooray!"

"Hip hip!"

"Hooray!"

"Hip hip!"

"Hooray!"

This was the weirdest day of Spyro's life.

"Thank you, my friends," said Kaos, the very words sounding strange coming out of his mouth. Kaos didn't have friends. He had minions and sworn enemies. "Now, spread the word. Wherever there is peril, wherever there is trouble, you can depend on Kaos to save the day. Kaos the champion. Kaos the hero. From this day on, evildoers are doomed, I tell you. DOOMED!"

Kaos threw his arms into the air and the two Mabu vanished in a flash of light.

"No!" Spyro gasped. "What have you done with them?"

"Er, he's just sent them home," explained Glumshanks.

"Back to where they belong," confirmed Kaos. "What did you think I would do with them?"

Spyro didn't know what to think.

"The question is, Skylanders, what to do with you?" Kaos continued.

Spyro's head snapped up. Kaos had walked over to Stealth Elf and was peering down at her sleeping form.

"Leave her alone," Spyro yelled, struggling back to his feet only to flop down again.

"Two of Eon's greatest Skylanders reduced to this. So weak." A sly grin played across his thin lips. "So helpless. So weak."

Finally, Spyro thought, *this is the Kaos we all know and hate.* It *was* a trap after all. He braced himself for the worst.

Kaos swept his arm through the air. "We can't have that. Summon the refreshing healing rain of VIBRANT VITALITY!"

Thunder rumbled above their heads and sweet-smelling rain started to fall. It splashed down on Spyro's scales, washing off the toad spit.

Beside Kaos, Stealth Elf stretched and yawned, waking to the feel of the cool water on her skin. She looked around, suddenly alert.

"Spyro? What's happening?"

Spyro shook his head. "I honestly have no idea."

Stealth looked up to see Kaos standing above her. Instantly, she reached for her daggers, but Kaos didn't even flinch. The Portal Master just sniffed at the beautiful orchid that was pinned to his lapel. Spyro hadn't noticed it before. Another mystery. Kaos hated all things natural. Why would he wear a flower?

"There's nothing to fear," Kaos said, smiling at Stealth—not a sneer or a leer, but what looked scarily like a genuine smile. "This is just the beginning of a beautiful friendship."

And with that, Kaos clapped his hands and Spyro found himself tumbling back into a Portal. Before he knew what

was happening, he was standing in Eon's citadel, staring at the expectant faces of Eon, Drill Sergeant, and Hugo.

"Well," prompted the Portal Master, as Stealth Elf materialized beside Spyro. "What happened?"

"It's Kaos," began Stealth, and a shadow fell over her friends at the sound of their archenemy's name.

"I knew it!" shouted Hugo, his glasses steaming up in fury. "What has the fiend done now?"

"Is he behind the monster attack?" Eon asked.

"No," said Spyro. "It's worse than that."

"Did he attack you, sir?" fumed Drill Sergeant.

Spyro shook his head.

"You don't understand. He saved us. Kaos has turned over a new leaf!"

Chapter Six

A CALL FoR HELP

"Ugh," moaned Spyro. "Three days of taking that stuff and it still doesn't taste any better."

Eon smiled and pushed the cork back into the bottle of healing elixir.

"The effects of the toad's saliva were serious, Spyro. Kaos may have washed the majority off your scales, but much of the damage had already been done." Eon tucked the smoky blue bottle back into his sleeve. "I shudder to think what would have happened to you and Stealth Elf if Kaos hadn't arrived when he did."

Spyro stretched out his wings and

gave them a few experimental flaps, rising gracefully from the floor. It may have tasted like troll dung, but Eon's elixir was doing the trick. He felt stronger than ever.

"It still doesn't seem right," Spyro said, dropping back to the stone slabs of the Portal chamber, "being saved by Kaos."

"Quite right, old chap," agreed Jet-Vac, who was enjoying the warmth of the Core of Light against his gray feathers. "*We* save other people from him!"

Eon sighed and gazed over at the stained glass windows that lined the room, lost in thought. "Perhaps it's true. Perhaps he has decided to mend his ways."

Spyro gasped.

"You can't really believe that, Master?"

Eon peered down sadly at his Skylander. The Portal Master was looking older than ever. "These days I don't know what to believe."

"Master Eon! Master Eon!"

Eon rolled his eyes at the sound of Hugo's voice. Spyro glanced over to see the little librarian bumbling into the chamber.

"Yes, Hugo. How can I help you?"

"I need to speak to you, Master. It's a matter of grave importance."

"Isn't it always?" Eon shared a sideways smile with Spyro, before his face fell. He closed his eyes, his brow furrowing.

"I found something in the cellar, Master. Something that really shouldn't be there. Something that—"

Eon raised a hand, silencing Hugo instantly.

"Something that will have to wait. Drill Sergeant is requesting a Portal."

Spyro looked up in surprise. "He's finished his mission? Already?"

"Let's find out."

Spyro and Jet-Vac scampered after Eon as he approached the Portal. Drill Sergeant had been sent to the Giggling Forest, a dense woodland where the trees laughed all day. However, they hadn't found the appearance of a gigantic sheep so funny, especially when it started to munch its way through their leaves. Mega toads and now mega sheep. There had to be a connection.

The Portal blazed into life and Drill Sergeant appeared in its center. He did not look happy. Hugo was the first to speak up.

"Well, don't just stand there. Were the rumors true? Was there really a . . ." the nervous Mabu's voice failed him.

Jet-Vac rolled his eyes. "Oh, good

grief. Put the pip-squeak out of his misery, Drill Sergeant. Was there a monster sheep or not?"

The bulldozer trundled off the platform, the light from the windows reflecting against his freshly repainted metal.

"Bop-de-bop. Not exactly."

Hugo relaxed. "Oh, thank goodness for that. It's bad enough that those bilious balls of walking wool are allowed to wander wherever they want. The thought of one the size of a small castle . . . well, it doesn't bear thinking about." Spyro shook his head, preparing for another of Hugo's rants. No one knew why, but Eon's assistant hated sheep. Actually, that was an understatement. Hugo detested sheep. He abhorred them. If he had his way, they would be wiped off the face of Skylands. While everyone else knew they were just stupid creatures that existed only to graze on grass, Hugo believed they were planning to take over the universe. That was why Trigger Happy liked nothing better than to hide a sheep or two in Hugo's wardrobe most weekends. The terrified Mabu's screams could be heard three islands away.

"Beep-be-beep. There wasn't one giant sheep," Drill Sergeant reported matter-of-factly.

"Good."

"Boop. There were two!"

"Two?" Hugo squeaked.

"Two?" Hugo squealed.

"TWO?" Hugo screamed as he ran full pelt from the Portal Chamber. Spyro suspected he was heading to hide under his bed. He also wondered what his reaction would be when he found the lamb that Trigger Happy had hidden under there earlier that day.

Eon chuckled and turned his attention

back to the Arkeyan bulldozer.

"What happened, Drill Sergeant? Did you save the forest?"

"Boop-bo-boop. I didn't get a chance, sir," Drill Sergeant replied, his gears grinding in frustration. "I was revving up for a power charge, ready to send the first mountain of mutton flying into next week, when *he* arrived."

"Who?"

With a snarl, Spyro answered for Drill Sergeant. "Kaos."

"Be-beep. That's right, sir." Spyro hated it when Drill Sergeant called him sir. Not that he could help it. Thousands of years ago, Drill Sergeant had been constructed by the ancient Arkeyans to bore through their diamond mines. He had been programmed to obey orders. Today, as a valued member of the Skylanders, he was a free machine, answering to no one, but old habits die hard. "Appeared out of nowhere he did, sir, waved that new staff of his and the sheep vanished, just like that. When I left, the trees were on their thirteenth rendition of 'For He's a Jolly Good Fellow.'"

"I keep hearing the same story from all over Skylands," admitted Eon, stroking his beard. "Yesterday, I sent Eruptor to save Flowering Fields from a five-meter-long caterpillar, only to find that Kaos had chased off the gigantic grub."

"And don't forget the colossal cockroach that was menacing Lucky Lagoon," Jet-Vac added, his beak curling down in disgust. "Kaos had sent it scuttling long before Hex and Cynder arrived on the scene."

Eon nodded sadly. "It's true. Whether we believe it or not, Kaos is rapidly becoming the hero of the hour."

"Well, I don't believe it," insisted Spyro. "Kaos is as evil as they come. This is a man who would give candy to a baby just so he could steal it back again."

"Spyro's right." Jet-Vac crossed his powerful arms across his chest. "That scoundrel wouldn't know a good deed if one came up and bopped him on the nose. He really ruffles my feathers."

"And yet," Eon pointed out, "it appears to be true. Perhaps we should accept that—"

"Help! Help!"

Uh-oh, Spyro thought. *Hugo's found the sheep beneath his bed.* But the cry wasn't coming from Hugo's bedroom. It was coming from the Portal.

Eon spun around and rushed back up the steps, placing his hand palm-down against the stone.

"It's coming from the Desert of Columns," he said, focusing in on the cries.

"The Desert of what, sir?" Drill Sergeant asked.

Spyro knew exactly where Eon meant. "The Desert of Columns is a mysterious and ancient plain. It is covered with incredibly tall columns that stretch into the clouds."

"No one knows how high the columns reach," Eon added. "Only one man has ever tried to climb them."

"Yes, but he disappeared from sight seventeen years ago," Spyro recalled. "No one knows how far he got. People say they are never-ending."

"That may be true," Eon said gravely, shifting his hand on the surface of the Portal. "But they are now under attack. Listen."

"It's a monster!" cried the voice from the Portal. "A huge, hideous monster."

"We must help them," Spyro cried out, spreading his wings, ready for action. Eon shook his head.

"No, Spyro. You are not fully recovered. Drill Sergeant and Jet-Vac will go."

"Beep-beepity-beep. Of course, sir. I'll leave immediately."

"You can count on us," added Jet-Vac, drawing his vacuum gun. "Ready to fight beak and claw. Tallyho!"

Spyro's wings drooped. He couldn't just sit back and rest while others needed help.

"Please," the voice pleaded. "Help us, Kaos. You're our only hope."

Spyro felt his skin crawl at the sound of his archenemy's name. Only hope, indeed. He shot a look at Eon, who sighed even as he activated the Portal.

"Very well, you may go as well. Just please, be careful."

Spyro bounded into the light.

Chapter Seven

THE DESERT OF COLUMNS

"Boop. Watch out, sir!"

Spyro's head snapped up to see a huge chunk of stone spinning through the air. It was heading toward the exact point at which Eon's Portal had deposited them. He breathed in. Perhaps he could deflect it with a fireball?

He didn't need to. The lump of masonry exploded into dust just above their heads. Beside him, a thin wisp of smoke curled from the auto-blaster mounted on Drill Sergeant's head.

"Good shooting, Drills," Spyro commented, impressed. He always liked working with the Arkeyan bulldozer. Nothing seemed to phase him.

"Be-beep. Thank you, sir."

"Please don't call me sir."

"Sorry, I'll try to remember, sir."

Another slab of rock landed near them, sending up a plume of sand. Spyro threw up a paw to protect his eyes.

"Heads up," Jet-Vac cried out, pointing through the dust. "Someone's coming."

Sure enough, a Molekin was running toward them, dodging falling rubble and waving his arms above his head in alarm.

"Thank goodness you've come. Thank you. Thank you so much."

Spyro recognized the voice. So this was who had called for help. Diggs had accompanied them on many of their adventures. Like all Molekin, he was hardworking, diligent, and, as he spent most of his time underground, wasn't blessed with the best of eyesight.

"Diggs," Spyro called out, "don't worry, we're here now. Where is the monster?"

The Molekin skidded to a halt, his face falling.

"Oh, sorry. I couldn't see who it was." He pushed his thick glasses back up his nose. "I thought you were Kaos."

Spyro suppressed a snarl. "You sound disappointed."

"No, no, not at all," insisted Diggs. "I've been helping with an archaeological dig of the entire area, or rather I was until that thing attacked the camp."

"Boop. What thing, sir?" asked Drill Sergeant.

"I think he means *that* thing," Jet-Vac answered, his beak hanging open as a shadow fell over them.

It was huge. Bigger than any other creature Spyro had ever seen. Bigger even than the toad in the Stinky Swamp. It towered over them, silhouetted against the sun, but Spyro knew exactly what it was from the shape of its huge flapping ears.

It was a troll. A massive, monstrous troll.

And not any old troll. Spyro squinted his eyes against the sun's glare. Ignoring the fact that this troll was larger than any troll ought to be, it was lanky, with great gangly legs and arms flailing around. Most trolls were squat little so-and-sos, but this one reminded him of someone. Someone he had last seen clutching a pair of shears.

"Does that thing remind you of someone?"

"Beep-be-be-beep. Not that I can tell, sir," Drill Sergeant replied, while Jet-Vac trained his sights on the huge creature.

"Does it matter?" the Air Skylander asked. "I'm more worried that it's heading this way!"

"Don't you see?" Spyro urged. "It's the spitting image of Glumshanks."

"Boop! Well, either he's grown, sir, or we've shrunk!"

The troll—whoever it was—stumbled forward. Instinctively, Spyro threw his wings over Diggs to protect the Molekin while Drill Sergeant and Jet-Vac took out the falling rubble with a volley of homing rockets and air blasts.

"Oi! Watch where you're firing those things. Waaaaaah!"

Spyro looked up at the sound of the voice to see a thin man with a long white beard and dressed in climbing equipment tumble out of the sky. Drill Sergeant had also spotted the old man and spun around to catch him.

"I don't believe it," yelled the elderly climber as he landed in Drill Sergeant's arms. "Seventeen years I've been climbing that column. Seventeen years. I was nearly at the top!"

"Such a shame when things don't go according to plan, eh, Skylander?"

Another new voice, this time to Spyro's right. The dragon spun around to see Kaos standing on the stump of a nearby column, brandishing that scarlet staff of his. "Bet you thought you were going to save the day, dragonfly?" The bald Portal Master giggled. "Well, get in line, fools! This one's mine!"

Kaos lunged forward with his staff before nearly overbalancing and tumbling from his column. He let out a frightened squeak and wobbled precariously, arms windmilling, before regaining his balance. Beside Spyro, Jet-Vac couldn't resist a snort of laughter. "Some hero," he whispered. Kaos cleared his throat, straightened the orchid in his lapel, and tried again, thrusting his staff up toward the gigantic troll.

"Stop in the name of KAOS!"

The huge troll froze where it was, throwing his hands back in alarm.

"Oh no," it boomed. "It is that heroic and oh-so-handsome Kaos." Something about its voice didn't sound right. It was as if it was reciting a speech. Badly. "I'm doomed. Doomed, I tell you."

The troll took a step back, nudging another column with its shoulder. Debris rained down once again, this time taking out the stump that Kaos was perched on top of. The Portal Master let out a pathetic squawk and pitched forward, tumbling to the ground. For a split second, Spyro considered letting him land headfirst in the sand, before leaping forward. He was a Skylander. Doing such a thing would make him no better than Kaos himself. Or at least the *old* Kaos.

Spyro leaped into the air, grabbing Kaos midplummet and lowering him to the ground. Kaos shrugged off Spyro's claws, and turned on the huge troll, his face purple with fury.

"What do you think you're doing, you clodhopping imbecile?" he bellowed into the air. "You could have hit me!"

"Sorry, Mast—" apologized the giant, before stopping himself. "I mean, RARGH! I'm going to squash you beneath my feet!"

Spyro gasped as the giant lifted one of its gargantuan feet and began to bring it down on top of them. He glanced around, making sure Drill Sergeant was out of trouble, but the bulldozer was still being berated by the furious climber. Jet-Vac was already swinging up his cannon, but Spyro knew that not even the Sky Baron's vacuum blasts would stop something that big. It was up to him. Spyro felt the fire ignite in his belly. If ever there was a time for a Daybringer Flame, it was now.

But he didn't have a chance. With a defiant cry, Kaos thrust his staff into the air, sending a blast of energy up into the bottom of the enormous foot. Spyro heard the troll shout out, "Oooh, that tickles," before it vanished with a deafening crack.

"Ha!" shouted Kaos triumphantly into the air. "That's what you get when you try to squash Kaos! I am victorious. AGAIN!"

"No," yelled Spyro, stalking toward the Portal Master. Despite his bravado, the dragon saw Kaos swallow hard and take a step back. "You're up to something. I know you are."

"Up to something?" Kaos said, recovering his composure and trying his very hardest to look innocent. "Little old me? Spyro, I'm hurt. I thought we were friends now, what with me saving your life and all."

"You can't fool us, Kaos."

"Indeed," Jet-Vac agreed, turning his hawk eyes on the Portal Master. "That was no ordinary troll."

Kaos let out a snort.

"No kidding, FOOL! I don't know if you noticed, Skychumps, but it was a mega troll!"

"No, it was Glumshanks," Spyro insisted.

Kaos's snort turned into a snigger.

"Glumshanks? You think that was Glumshanks? That huge, stompy monster?"

The snigger turned into a belly laugh.

"Bwa-ha-ha-haaaaa. I knew you were stupid, but . . ."

"Has someone cracked a joke, Master?"

Spyro's head snapped around. It was

Glumshanks shuffling around a boulder, covered in dust and sand.

"Glummy old pal, old chum, old friend," screamed Kaos, pulling his butler into a bear hug, his voice dripping with concern. "Where have you been?"

Spyro had never seen Glumshanks look so uncomfortable. He wasn't used to his master being nice to him.

"Er, I got caught beneath that boulder when the . . . er . . . mega troll knocked over a column. I had to dig myself out."

"You poor thing," fawned Kaos, never taking his eyes off Spyro. "Let's get you home. Bye-bye, SKYLOSERS!"

Spyro could still see Kaos's smug smile, even after he'd conjured up a Portal to magic them away.

Brushing dust from his shoulders, Diggs tottered up to Spyro. "Oh dear. Has Kaos gone? I wanted to thank him."

Chapter Eight

DARKNESS FALLS

Stealth Elf was waiting for them when they returned to the Portal Chamber, and Trigger Happy hopping from one foot to the other in excitement now that they had returned. The gremlin always loved hearing about his friends' exploits. Stealth, on the other hand, could see something was wrong. She took one look at Spyro's face and frowned.

"Let me guess. Kaos?"

"There's only one thing worse than having your life saved by that odious little creep," snarled Spyro.

"Having it happen more than once?" Stealth suggested.

"You got it. I've never seen him looking so smug."

"What was it this time?" Trigger Happy asked excitedly. "A mammoth-size mouse? An elephantine ant?"

"It was worse than that, old girl." Jet-Vac hopped down from the Portal, followed closely by Drill Sergeant.

"Bop-bo-bop. Much worse." The Arkeyan whirred, turning toward Stealth Elf. "It was a towering troll, sir."

Stealth Elf's glowing eyes narrowed.

"Sir?" she spat, hands on hips. "Do I look like a sir?"

Drill Sergeant's gears whirred in panic as he realized his gaffe.

"Beep. Sorry, sir. Not at all, sir. My mistake, sir."

Noticing her rising anger, Jet-Vac placed a feathered arm around Stealth's shoulders. "My dear, trust me—some arguments just aren't worth having."

"Where's Master Eon?" Spyro asked, already starting across the chamber. "I need to talk to him. Drills is right. It was a huge troll, but also a very familiar one. I think I know what is happening."

"What is happening?" shrieked a voice from outside the door. Spyro skidded to a halt as Hugo careened across the threshold, his head in his hands. "Master Eon!"

"Hugo? What's wrong?"

"Spyro. Thank the Portals that you are here. Something dreadful has happened! Something awful!"

"Hugo, if this has something to do with sheep . . ." Spyro warned, throwing a glance at the sniggering Trigger Happy, but the little librarian shook his head so hard his glasses nearly flew off.

"No, it's worse than even that. Look!"

Hugo pointed at the stained glass windows with a shaking finger. Spyro followed his gaze and let out a gasp. Usually light streamed through the thousand-year-old glass, illuminating images of the Skylanders of old. The colors sparkled and danced across the Chamber's cold stone floor, brilliant blues, rich reds, and glorious greens. You could feel the heat of the sun on your skin wherever you stood.

Not today.

Today the windows were dark. Today the colors were dull and lifeless. Today a chill fell over the chamber.

The light had gone.

"Darkness has fallen!" wailed Hugo. "Darkness has fallen!"

The five of them ran outside, a thousand and one fears racing through Spyro's mind. Was it Kaos? Had he finally shown his true colors? Had he found a way to destroy the Core of Light? If Darkness had really fallen, what next? Spyro had read the warnings found in the ancient scrolls, the prophecies about what would happen if Darkness ever prospered. All light would be extinguished. Plants would wither and die. Birds would never sing again. The undead would inherit the land and the seas would turn to treacle. Okay, so that last one was a little bit farfetched, but Spyro didn't want to take any chances.

Whatever happened, he knew they would fight. The Skylanders would stop at nothing to bring back the light and . . .

His mouth dropped open when he saw what was outside the citadel, stopping so suddenly that Stealth Elf almost barreled into his back. Only her training stopped her crashing into him.

Hugo wasn't as nimble as the elf. He didn't notice that Drill Sergeant had slammed on his brakes, and he piled into the bulldozer with a clang. He bounced back and landed in a heap on the ground, his glasses skittering across the grass. Muttering to himself, the Mabu felt around for his specs and, finding them, pushed them back onto his nose. It was only then that he looked up and let out a quiet, mournful, "Oh!"

Darkness hadn't fallen. The Core of Light was still where it had always stood, but its beacon was hidden behind the massive airship that hung above the citadel.

The ship was huge, bigger than an entire flotilla of Drow Zeppelins, its jet-black hull casting a dark shadow over everything.

Weapons bristled across its flanks: cannons, harpoons, and guns jostling out of hundreds of portholes.

"Who are they?" Stealth Elf asked, her daggers already drawn—not that they would do much good against such a mighty warship. "The Drow?"

"I don't think so," Spyro replied honestly. "I've never seen a ship like it. Is it Arkeyan?"

Drill Sergeant's rockets were spinning on his arms, preparing to fire. "Be-beep. No, sir. My ancient masters built terrible weapons, but nothing like that."

"If it's not the Drow or the Arkeyans," Jet-Vac said, air cannon at the ready, "then who? Kaos?"

Hugo whimpered. "It's worse than that, I'm afraid."

"Worse than Kaos?" Trigger Happy positively beamed, reveling in the thought of a showdown with a new enemy.

Hugo nodded. "Yes. They're . . ."

His voice faltered.

"Yes?" prompted Spyro, sparks flying from his mouth.

"They're . . ."

"YES?"

"Librarians."

Spyro couldn't believe his ears. "Librarians?" he repeated, astonished.

"With a warship?" added Stealth Elf.

"And more weapons than a troll's birthday party?" finished Trigger Happy.

Hugo shuffled his feet. "They're very special librarians," he mumbled, embarrassed.

"Indeed they are," came a voice from behind them. Eon was standing in the doorway to the citadel, his eyes fixed on his assistant. "The Warrior Librarians of the Eternal Archives, keepers of the most dangerous books ever written. Archivists of forbidden knowledge. Curators of the arcane. The kind of people you don't want to cross."

He swept toward them, his face like thunder.

"What have you done?"

Hugo squirmed beneath his master's gaze.

"I tried to tell you, oh great one, but things kept getting in the way. This business with the mega monsters and Kaos. Spyro and Stealth Elf's injuries . . ."

"Hugo . . ."

The furry assistant plunged his hand into his light brown satchel.

"I found it when spring-cleaning the cellars, sir. It was at the bottom of a dusty crate." He pulled out a small, leather-bound book. "I must have borrowed it years ago. I—I thought I'd returned it."

Eon sighed, his shoulders sagging beneath his robes.

"A book from the Eternal Archive."

"Yes, Master."

"Where no books are supposed to leave."

"I know, Master. I'm sorry, Master."

"Show it to me." Eon held out a hand and took the thin volume from Hugo. He turned it over and looked at the title.

"What is it?" asked Spyro. "A book of spells?"

"Secret writings?" asked Stealth Elf.

"Ancient prophecies?" asked Drill Sergeant.

Eon shook his head. "I'm afraid not. Tell them, Hugo."

Hugo peered up at them over his glasses. "It's *101 Ways to Rid Yourself of Sheep and Other Wooly Nuisances*." He shuffled his feet in the grass. "Volume Two."

Spyro groaned. Typical.

"It wasn't even very good," Hugo continued. "Someone had ripped out the last page."

Before anyone could say anything, a trapdoor opened in the keel of the Librarians' airship. Three ropes tumbled down, their long ends piling up on the ground in front of the Skylanders.

"Oh no!" Hugo whimpered, fighting the urge to run. "Here they come."

Sure enough, three bulky figures were sliding down the ropes, speeding toward them. Spyro crouched, ready for action. One by one, the Warrior Librarians hit the ground and stomped forward. They were immense, clad in intimidating silver armor from head to toe. Domed helmets with a single slit for eyes sat atop broad shoulders, the seal of the Eternal Archives emblazoned across their barrel chests. Powerful arms swayed as they marched in unison, each with a blaster gun mounted on one of their hands, an energy blade attached to the other.

They came to a halt, the tallest at the front. This one sported an elaborate crest on its chest, and a long purple cloak hung beneath wide shoulder

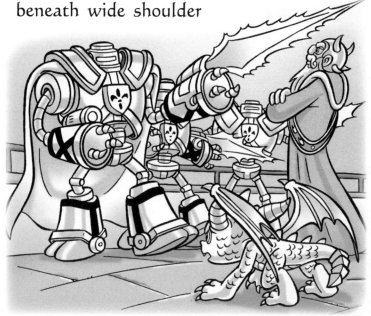

pads. It had to be the leader. Even its energy blade was bigger than the others, electric-blue lightning crackling along its length. It stood in silence.

No one spoke.

No one even dared to move.

Then, Eon stepped forward, holding his head high, and greeted the newcomers.

"Welcome, oh Warrior Librarians. How may we be of assistance?"

The leader of the group stared back at Eon, cocking its head. Its arms flexed, the sword sizzling in its hand, and then with the sound of tearing metal, a crack appeared down the middle of its capacious chest. Pistons hissed as the armor swung open like two great doors, steam gushing through the gap.

When the smoke cleared, Spyro couldn't believe what was sitting within the Librarian's terrifying torso.

Chapter Nine

THE ETERNAL ARCHIVES

"Greetings, Master Eon," wheezed a tiny voice. "It is good to see you again."

Eon's face broke into a dazzling smile.

"I don't believe it!" the Portal Master exclaimed, raising his hands in delight. "Chief Curator Wiggleworth, my old friend. How wonderful to see you."

Spyro and Stealth Elf glanced at each other, dumbstruck. Nestled in the middle of the hulking mechanical armor, curled up on what looked like an incredibly comfy chair,

sat a worm. Granted, it was a worm with a tiny gray beard, a large forehead, and massive glasses resting on its nose, but it still wasn't what Spyro had expected.

Behind Wiggleworth's armor, the chests of the other two Librarians were swinging open to reveal similar creatures. Each was no bigger than a banana and was surrounded by an array of pulleys and levers—obviously how they piloted their robotic suits.

"It is good to see you too, Eon," said Wiggleworth in his high, shrill voice. "I just wish it was in more pleasurable circumstances."

"Ah, yes," said Eon. "I believe my

assistant has something that belongs to you. Hugo?"

Hugo shuffled by Spyro and offered the small leather book to the chief curator. Wiggleworth squirmed in his chair, manipulating the controls. His suit of armor then reached down to pluck the tome from the Mabu's quaking hand. He peered through his thick glasses at the title page.

"*101 Ways to Rid Yourself of Sheep and Other Wooly Nuisances*. Oh, I wouldn't worry about that. Awful book. Plus, someone has ripped out the last page. You can keep it."

He tossed the book back down to Hugo, who fumbled to catch it and ended up falling backward into a flower bed.

"But if you're not here to collect the book . . ." Spyro began expectantly. Wiggleworth scrutinized Spyro with curious eyes.

"My, my. Is that who I think it is, Eon?"

The Portal Master nodded proudly, and a smile spread beneath Wiggleworth's bushy mustache.

"Spyro the Dragon. As I live and breathe. It's a pleasure to meet you, my young pup. A pleasure indeed. I've read so much about you. We all have."

Behind him, the other bookworms were nodding furiously.

"You've read about me?" Spyro asked, glancing up at Eon, unsure. "Where?"

"In the scrolls of the ancients," the Curator replied, writhing excitedly in his chair. "Your exploits are legendary. Skylands's greatest champion."

"They are?"

"Indeed. Absolutely thrilling. I've read all of them, tales of adventures past, present, and yet to come. You shall do astonishing things, Spyro. Astonishing things indeed."

Spyro felt himself blushing. He didn't know what to say.

"I never knew we had a celebrity in our midst," Jet-Vac whispered, raising his eyebrows.

"I shall have to remember to curtsy next time I see you, Spyro," teased Trigger Happy, grinning from ear to ear.

"Shut it, you two," hissed Spyro, embarrassed.

"I always said you chose your Skylanders well, Eon," continued Wiggleworth. "Yes indeed. A great judge of character. Which is why we need your help."

Eon's expression hardened, suddenly getting down to business.

"Of course, my friend. What do you need?"

"The Eternal Archive is in terrible danger, Eon. Our darkest hour. The Skylanders are our only hope."

Even though Spyro enjoyed traveling via Portal, there was nothing like soaring through the sky onboard an airship. The dragon stood at the prow of the Warrior Librarians' vast warship, his eyes closed, enjoying the wind rushing between his spines.

He had traveled on many such ships in his time, but nothing like this. The majestic ship thundered through the clouds, its twin propellers whirling at the stern, the vast purple balloon fastened firmly above their head. Its speed and agility were amazing for a vessel so large, and almost as soon as they had left Eon's citadel, Drill Sergeant had trundled off excitedly to explore the engine rooms. Like all Tech Skylanders, Drills was fascinated by machinery. Stealth Elf had stayed with Spyro, and even though, as a Life Skylander, she preferred to keep her feet firmly on the ground, he could tell she was enjoying the flight as much as he was. He opened his eyes to see her standing beside him, her blue hair blowing in the wind. Above them, Trigger Happy was hanging off one of the masts by his long tongue, like a crazy giggling flag.

The crank of gears and hiss of hydraulics told them that a Librarian was approaching. They turned to see Chief Curator

Wiggleworth's robot armor stomping toward them. The bookworm himself was safely enclosed within the armored chest now, protected from the elements. His cloak flapped in the breeze as he lumbered to a halt.

"I have sent my assistants down to retrieve your colleague from the engineering section," Wiggleworth said, his voice amplified through the armor's speaker system. "We are almost at our destination."

Proudly, Wiggleworth raised his robotic arms as the ship broke through the clouds. Spyro turned and grinned as he saw the island rushing toward them. "Behold, the Eternal Archive."

The great lump of rock hung in the sky, surrounded by smaller floating islands. It was covered by an awe-inspiring building. Marble towers rose majestically from behind a thick jewel-encrusted wall, each topped by a graceful onyx spire. They flew toward the sturdy-looking iron gates, which were emblazoned with the same emblem the Librarians wore on their robotic chests: a gigantic figure eight, the symbol for eternity.

You couldn't help but be impressed. Spyro whistled at the sheer scale of the place. He'd thought Eon's own library had been big until he had seen this. It was mind-boggling.

"Every book that has ever been published finds a home within our walls," Wiggleworth was explaining, obviously enjoying the look on the Skylanders' faces. "From every corner of the universe."

"But Master Eon said you look after the most dangerous books ever written," said Spyro, remembering the Portal Master's words.

"And he is right, as usual," Wiggleworth

replied gravely. "Deep with the bowels of the island, safe within our high-security vault, is our collection of the most terrible books creation has ever seen."

"As in badly written?" Stealth Elf asked.

"No, my dear." Spyro could imagine the bookworm within the armor shaking his head. "As in dark secrets and restricted knowledge. Powerful books. Magical books. Evil books. We have vowed to keep them safe for all eternity, so that they can never fall into the wrong hands."

Spyro could think of at least one pair of hands that would want that kind of knowledge, no matter how heroic he now appeared to be.

Kaos.

"But you still haven't explained why you need our help," Spyro said, feeling a cold shiver pass down his tail. "You said you were facing your darkest hour."

Wiggleworth didn't reply at first, but slipped his energy blade into its scabbard. He tapped at a set of controls embedded into his arm and opened a communication channel with the ship's captain.

"Captain, take us about the Archive. Our friends need to see the extent of our problem."

The deck lurched as the airship came about, the hull creaking with the change in air pressure. Spyro leaned to keep his balance, never taking his eyes from the Archive walls.

"Beep-be-be-beep. You should see the engines, sir," said Drill Sergeant, trundling up behind them. "Absolutely marvelous. All gleaming brass and . . ." His voice trailed off. "What are you all looking at?"

Spyro's heart was beating against his ribs. He couldn't speak. He could hardly move. Now it was obvious why the Warrior Librarians wanted their assistance.

"Oh," said Drill Sergeant as they cleared the walls and saw what was sitting next to the Archive.

"Oh indeed," repeated Wiggleworth.

There, in the gardens of the Archive, dwarfing the collection's massive walls, sat a gigantic, enormous, stupendously large Chompy Pod.

Chapter Ten

A BIG PROBLEM

The four Skylanders stood in the shadow of the Chompy Pod. The ship had docked beside the Archive and they had climbed down the gangplank in silence. All eyes were on the Pod, and all thoughts were on what was inside.

"So, how many Chompies can come out of a normal-size Chompy Pod?" asked Trigger Happy, his tongue lolling out of the side of his gaping mouth as he tried to take in the scale of the plant.

"Four or five at first," Stealth Elf replied, "although leave it unchecked and it'll keep spewing them out for all time."

"Be-be-beep. And how much damage can four or five Chompies do?"

"They could eat through a field of grain in five minutes flat if you let them," replied Spyro.

"Thought so, sir," said Drill Sergeant quietly. "Thank you, sir."

"So let me get this straight," Trigger continued, absently playing with the safety catches on his golden guns. "The average

Chompy comes up to your knee."

"Yes," said Spyro.

"Knees they'll instantly try to bite off."

"Yes," said Spyro.

"And this Chompy Pod, it must be, what, eight stories high."

This time Spyro didn't reply. He was too busy imagining the size of the Chompies growing inside.

Trigger Happy whistled. "Just think of the teeth . . ."

"We've thrown everything we have at it," explained Wiggleworth, stepping forward from the battalion of Warrior Librarians that had traipsed off the ship. "Cannons, catapults, battering rams, and blaster rays. Nothing has even left a mark on it. Of course, we're not so much worried about the Pod . . ."

"Rather, what happens when the Chompies themselves hatch," said Spyro, completing the chief curator's sentence.

"And what carnage they will cause," Stealth Elf added.

"Exactly. Three, four, maybe even five giant Chompies running around? They could chew through the Archive's walls in minutes. No book on our shelves would be safe. All those treasures would be lost forever."

"Be-beep. And then there's the vault, sir," reminded Drill Sergeant. "Don't forget the vault."

"As if I could. We just have to find a way to destroy the Pod before it hatches."

It was almost as if the impossible plant was listening to the chief curator's words. As if on cue, the Pod shuddered, a deep, sickening gurgle bubbling up from behind its thick emerald skin.

Stealth Elf's hands went to the hilts of her daggers.

"It won't be long," she said, her voice buzzing with urgency. "They've started to break out."

"Then we need to act," Spyro shouted, beating his wings and rising into the air above their heads. "Curator, have your Librarians train their weapons on the Pod."

Behind them, twenty Warrior Librarians moved as one, bringing their blasters up to target the plant.

"Drills, start your engines."

The bulldozer raised his arms, drill bits already revolving. "Boop-boop. DX3000-Detonators ready for firing, sir."

"Stealth, summon your shadowsbane blades."

Stealth Elf threw up her arms, muttering an elven incantation

behind her mask. The air shimmered around her as three spinning blades formed out of nowhere, dancing around her, waiting to attack.

"Trigg, lock and load."

The gremlin didn't need to be told twice. His guns were already covering the gigantic target.

Spyro turned back to the plant, feeling the fire ignite in his own belly. This was it. Now or never. He opened his mouth and cried, "Fire!"

The noise was tremendous. Twenty energy bolts sliced through the air. Drill Sergeant's drill rockets erupted from his arms. Stealth Elf's enchanted blades whirled forward, slashing at the tough green hide, and Trigg fired round after round of shining ammo, the golden gunfire almost drowning out his peals of excited laughter.

Spyro joined in the assault, a volley of

fireballs blazing from his open mouth.

But it didn't work.

The blaster bolts slammed helplessly against the Pod.

The drill bits exploded to little effect.

The blades blunted against the chunky skin.

The golden coins tumbled back to the ground.

The fireballs bounced back at Spyro.

The Pod wasn't even singed.

"Cease firing," Spyro reluctantly cried, dropping back to the ground. "It's no good."

"Beep. Do we have a plan B, sir?" asked Drill Sergeant, new drill rockets automatically constructing at the ends of his arms.

"Or even a plan C, D, or E?" added Trigger Happy.

"I'm open to suggestions," Spyro admitted, looking up at the Pod in despair.

"Well, whatever we do, I suggest we do it quick," insisted Stealth Elf, her now-useless blades fading away. "That thing is about to blow."

Sure enough, the Pod was writhing and gurgling, its green skin stretching as the creatures within struggled to get out.

With a wet, squelching rip and a plume of pungent spores, the Pod split and five very tall and very hungry Chompies burst out of its leaves.

Chapter Eleven

HUGE APPETITES

If their weapons had little effect on the Pod, they were next to useless on the Chompies themselves. The five monsters charged forward, looking for something to eat, looking for anything to eat. One started to rip trees out of the ground as if they were daisies, while another set its sights on the airship. The remaining two piled straight into the wall. Bricks and gems rained down to the ground as their diamond-hard teeth made short work of the Archive's defenses.

The Warrior Librarians that managed to avoid being trampled underfoot were firing salvo after salvo at the creatures, although their blasts were close to useless. It was like gnats snapping at a rhinoceros.

Drill Sergeant had given up trying to blast the Chompies with his drill rockets and instead kept thundering forward in power charges, ramming their feet. He bounced off every time like a rubber ball.

Spyro swooped down to find his friend flailing around hopelessly on his back.

"Be-beep! How embarrassing can this get, sir?" Drill Sergeant complained as Spyro helped him back on his tracks. "I've tunneled through mountains and excavated volcanoes and yet can't knock a simple Chompy off its feet."

"There's nothing simple about this Chompy," shouted Spyro, soaring back into the air and narrowly missing a tumbling lump of masonry. "About any of them."

Spyro heard a cry from below. He look down to see Stealth Elf trapped beneath one of the Chompies' feet. She was jabbing its ankle with her daggers, trying to get it to shift, but the thing didn't even flinch. Trigg had abandoned his guns and was desperately trying to help, shoving against the leg for all his worth. Spyro pulled his wings in close and fell into a dive, dropping his horns into optimum butting position.

Wham!

He slammed into the Chompy's ankle and ricocheted off in the opposite direction. He hit the ground with a grunt and tumbled head over tail before finally coming to a halt. His head spun, stars dancing across his vision. Skylands's greatest champion? Ha!

He wondered what Wiggleworth thought of him now.

Swerving to avoid the pounding feet of another marauding Chompy, Spyro tore back over to where Stealth Elf was trapped. He grabbed her arm in his jaws and heaved. It was no good. No matter how hard he pulled, she was stuck fast, and the Chompy was showing no sign of shifting. It was too busy gnawing through the wall.

"Stay there," Spyro barked at Stealth Elf, and shot back into the air.

"Where else am I going to go?" she shouted after him. "This is quite a pressing engagement."

Spyro wasn't listening. He was flying straight up the side of the Chompy, past its massive mouth, past its gleaming white teeth, over its drawn-back lips, and up to its beady black eyes. Eyes that were each the size of a hot air balloon. They swayed hungrily at the top of thick antenna, staring hungrily ahead, imagining what tasty treats lay beyond the wall.

Spyro came in level with the eyes and yelled at the top of his voice.

"Hey, fang features! Over here."

The eyes swiveled, finally focusing on the tiny dragon. The creature roared. It wasn't the shrill squeak you usually associate with a Chompy, but a terrifying explosion of noise. It was so loud it almost blasted Spyro into the wall, but his tired wings pounded the air, keeping him hovering in front of the beast.

Spyro didn't mind admitting he was scared. Who wouldn't be? But he needed that fear. It would help him focus on what he was about to do.

He sucked air into his lungs and felt flames burst into life inside his belly. He closed his eyes, fueling the fire, stoking

it, letting it rage almost out of control. Then, when it felt as if he could no longer contain it, he breathed out. The fireball that erupted from his mouth was the biggest and brightest he'd ever produced.

The Daybringer Flame.

Searing white light flooded over the island, illuminating everything for miles around. Only Spyro could look directly into the inferno. Only Spyro saw the Chompy recoil, temporarily blinded by the brightness of the light. It stumbled back, stumpy arms waving in confusion, teeth grinding against one another.

Then it was gone, tumbling over the edge of the island, plunging down into the void below.

Spyro didn't waste time. He plummeted down to where Stealth Elf lay, at the edge of a huge Chompy footprint. She was blinking madly, trying to clear her vision, while Trigger Happy bounced up and down on the spot, cheering loudly.

"Next time you have a bright idea," she laughed, pulling herself to her feet, "tell me so I can close my eyes first."

Then she winced as she tried to put weight on her ankle, leaning heavily on Spyro.

"You're hurt," Spyro yelled over the sound of the battle. "You should call for a Portal."

"Never!" she called back. "You think I'm going to let you get all the glory? I'll be—"

Stealth Elf never completed her sentence. None of the Skylanders had noticed the angry Chompy swinging its leg toward them, but they definitely felt it as the vengeful creature booted them high into the air. Spyro looked up in horror to see that they were all flying straight into the gaping mouth of another giant Chompy.

Chapter Twelve

KAOS TO THE RESCUE

Drill Sergeant watched as his three friends arced toward the monster's grinning mouth, Trigg's tongue trailing behind them like a demented ribbon.

"Boop. Oh no, you don't," the bulldozer beeped, his eyes closing to small dots. "If you want something to chomp on, try this."

With a grunt of effort, he plunged both of his revolving drill bits into the soft ground, anchoring them into the earth. When he was sure they were secure, he fired the rockets. With nowhere to go, the

blast shot the Skylander into the air. He whizzed up, wheels spinning, blaster firing in all directions.

"Beep-beep. I hope you know a good dentist," Drill Sergeant roared as he slammed into one of the Chompy's massive fangs. There was a bone-splintering crunch, and the tooth was knocked clear from the creature's gums. It wailed, instinctively closing its mouth. Instead of flying straight down its gullet, Spyro and Stealth Elf smacked into its lips and tumbled to the floor. Just before they hit the ground, Spyro righted himself, grabbed Stealth, and spread his wings wide so that the two of them would glide to safety. As soon as they were down, he ran across to Drill Sergeant, who had landed on his head, and flipped him the right way up with his horns.

"Bo-bop. Most obliged, sir," Drill

Sergeant said. "The oil was rushing to my head."

"No, it's you we've got to thank," Spyro insisted as Stealth Elf hobbled over. "We nearly became a Chompy snack."

Above them, the defanged Chompy was still wailing in agony. Spyro's smile faded as he realized what was about to happen, but there was nothing he could do. Blinded with pain, the Chompy stumbled back, stood on its own dislodged tooth, leaped up in shock, and fell back into the Archive walls. The beleaguered defenses could take no more and collapsed, sending bricks flying everywhere.

That was it. The Chompies were in the Archive. They would munch their way through every book and there was little anyone could do. Spyro looked around. Most of the Librarians had been crushed under the Chompies' feet, and those that were left were gently rescuing the other bookworms from mangled armor. Stealth Elf had a busted ankle, Drill Sergeant still looked dazed, and Trigg's guns were still on the other side of the green.

"We need reinforcements," Spyro shouted.

"I thought you'd never ask," came an all-too-familiar voice. Spyro's heart sank as he whirled around to greet the newcomer.

It was Kaos, with Glumshanks cowering behind his master's flapping robes.

"What do you want?" Spyro growled, rounding on his nemesis.

"What do I want?" Kaos sneered. "I,

Kaos, champion of the oppressed, righter of wrongs?" He wrinkled his nose in disgust. "I want you to stand aside, Skyblunderer, and let a real hero get to work."

With a flourish, Kaos pointed his staff at the wounded Chompy, which was still lying in the ruins of the Archive. There was a familiar crackle of energy and the monster vanished.

The remaining three Chompies didn't care. They were already charging for the gap in the wall.

"Oh deary, deary me, this is dreadful. Disastrous." Spyro looked up to see Wiggleworth being carried in the palm of a distinctly battered-looking Warrior Librarian. The chief curator's own suit had been reduced to a sparking wreck during the first attack. "Our walls have been breached. You must do something, Spyro. Please."

"Look who it is," jeered Kaos, peering

down at the worm. "Chief Curator Wiggleworth. Long time no see."

The worm gazed up in bewilderment, obviously none the wiser.

"I'm sorry, but have we met?"

"I thought you said everyone knew who you were, Master? That you were now the most famous champion of Skylands?" commented Glumshanks, receiving a sharp elbow in the ribs in response.

"It was a long time ago, when I was a child," Kaos continued, smirking horribly. "I wanted to borrow *World Domination for Beginners*. You said it wasn't available for loan. The same went for *The Complete A to Z of Being Diabolical*. 'Reference only,' you said."

"And I was right," blustered the Curator, his mustache bristling. "They must never leave the Archive's walls."

"Those walls?" questioned Kaos,

jabbing a stumpy finger at the pile of bricks where the defenses used to be. "The walls being attacked by humongous Chompies?" He gestured with his thumb toward the approaching monsters, who suddenly floated slightly off the ground. Their eyes boggled in shock and their legs wiggled as they bobbed in midair. "The Chompies

I have now trapped in my lighter-than-air levitation spell?"

Wiggleworth let out a huge sigh of relief.

"Oh, thank you. Thank you, thank you, thank you."

"Don't mention it," hissed Kaos. "I suppose you'll be wanting me to get rid of them now? Would that help?"

The worm nodded, his cracked glasses bouncing up and down on his nose.

"That would be marvelous. We would be forever in your debt."

Kaos grinned, revealing a row of yellowing, uneven teeth.

"Excellent. You see, there is the little matter of my payment . . ."

Now Spyro had heard everything. "Payment?" he repeated, incredulous. "You're expecting the Librarians to pay you? What about being a hero?"

A look of mock outrage flickered over

Kaos's smarmy features.

"Heroes still have to eat, don't they? What do you think I am? A charity?"

"But we can't pay," Wiggleworth stammered. "We don't have any money. We only deal in books."

Kaos's forehead crinkled into a frown.

"Only in books you say, hmmmm." He tapped a stubby finger against his chin. "Glumshanks, give me the paper . . ."

The troll looked up at his master expectantly.

"Master?"

"The paper, Glumshanks. The very important paper I gave you on the off chance that the Warrior Librarians of the Eternal Archive only dealt in books."

"Oh, that paper!" Glumshanks exclaimed, digging around in his tatty tunic. After a few seconds of groping, he produced a scrunched up piece of paper and handed it to his master.

"One of these days, Glumshanks . . ." Kaos warned, snatching the paper and thrusting it toward the bookworm. "Here. You will get me this book or I'll release the Chompies."

"That's blackmail!" Spyro stated, although he shouldn't have been surprised. Kaos had done much worse in the past.

"Such an ugly word, dragonfly," Kaos sneered. "A correct one, I'll grant you, but ugly all the same."

Wiggleworth looked at the paper and his face went pale.

"No," he whispered. "That is not possible."

"You dare defy me, fool? You dare defy Kaos? Your savior?"

"You don't understand. That book is in the vault. It's forbidden."

"Believe me, I understand perfectly."

Kaos wiggled his thumb. "Your choice, small fry. Deliver the book into my hands or your precious library is doomed." He leaned closer to the curator, his piggy nose inches from Wiggleworth's own. "DOOOOMED!"

Wiggleworth brought himself up to his (quite unimpressive) full height and held his chin high. "Never!"

Kaos sighed and rolled his eyes.

"Oh, very well. Don't say I, Kaos, didn't warn you. MINIONS! EAT UP! Ha-ha-ha-haaaa!"

With a flick of his wrist, Kaos's spell was broken, and the three giant Chompies dropped back to the ground and raced for the breach in the wall.

Chapter Thirteen

TRUE COLORS

The Chompies bared their gigantic teeth as they raced forward. As Trigger Happy whipped out his extraordinarily long tongue to recover his golden pistols, Drill Sergeant sent a barrage of homing rockets flying up to meet them, but they did little damage.

Kaos, meanwhile, was cackling with laughter as Wiggleworth moaned in dismay. Spyro hated to admit it, but Kaos was the only person who could defeat these things, as he had defeated all the other mega monsters that had appeared recently.

Then he caught something out of the

corner of his eye. A tiny Chompy was staggering out of the ruins of the wall. A small, regular-size Chompy. A Chompy that was missing a tooth.

Even as Trigger Happy frantically squeezed off another half-dozen rounds of gold coins, everything became clear. Kaos hadn't destroyed the giant Chompy that Drill Sergeant had defanged. He'd just shrunk it down to its normal size. Why? Because the little twerp had been the one who had made it so big in the first place.

"Stealth, first question: can you walk?" Spyro hissed through clenched teeth.

"I can run if it helps stop those things."

"Good. Second question: can you get Kaos's staff?"

Ignoring her aching ankle, Stealth Elf was off like a shot. She moved so fast she was a blur. Before Kaos knew what hit him, she had grabbed the red staff and was standing back at Spyro's side. "You mean this one?"

"Wha . . . ," screamed Kaos, staring at his empty hands. "Give that back to me!"

"I don't think so," shouted Spyro, shooting into the air. "Steath Elf, supersize me!"

Stealth Elf pointed the staff at Spyro and a beam of magical energy shot toward the dragon. It hit him square in the chest, and, in the blink of an eye, Spyro was the size of the giant Chompies. A second later, he was twice as big again.

"That's more like it!" the mega Spyro roared, his voice rattling every window in the Archive. "It's time you three picked on someone your own size."

The Chompies skidded to a halt, but still bared their fangs. This was going to be a big scrap.

Spyro flapped his mighty wings, each beat like a thunderclap, and soared up into the sky. He pivoted in midair and plunged back down, butting into the first Chompy. It sailed off its feet, through the air, and over the edge of the island.

"One down. Two to go!" Spyro boomed, before letting out a shriek of pain. One of the other Chompies had bitten down on his tail and was holding fast.

At ground level, Stealth Elf gasped, momentarily distracted by the fight. It was all Kaos needed.

"I'll take that, fool." Without warning, he grabbed the staff and jabbed it at Stealth Elf. The crystal on the end lit up and, for a moment, Drill Sergeant thought his friend had been disintegrated. Then he heard a tiny, weenie voice.

"Down here!" it cried. "Down here!"

The bulldozer peered down to see a minuscule Stealth Elf in the grass. Kaos had shrunk her to the size of an ant.

The evil Portal Master pointed the staff at Spyro. "Time to bring you down to size, you COLOSSAL CRETIN!" he cried, letting loose a beam of light. Spyro saw the crystal flare and, straining with the weight of the Chompy, swung his tail around. The Chompy was pulled off its feet, straight into the path of the beam. With a flash and a squeak, it was reduced to its usual dimensions and thudded to the floor, stunned.

"Bah! I won't miss this time, fool!" Kaos screamed, bringing the staff about. Spyro opened his mouth to breathe a ball of fire at the Portal Master, but needn't have bothered.

"Yow!" shrieked Kaos, leaping into the air. "That really hurt!"

Drill Sergeant's eyebrows shot up as he watched the Portal Master hop around clutching his ankle. Then he noticed something stuck deep in Kaos's ankle—a teensy dragonfang dagger buried right up to its handle. The pin-size Stealth Elf had taken her revenge.

Kaos scratched at his ankle, trying to pull the dagger out, yelping all the time. "Get it out! Get it out!"

Glumshanks ran over to his master and grabbed Kaos's ankle, sending the bald villain crashing onto his back with a thud. "You're always giving yourself splinters," the troll butler tutted before expertly plucking the dagger from his skin.

Kaos sighed in relief before his face fell.

"Missing something?" thundered Spyro as he wrestled with the remaining Chompy. Kaos's eyes went wide.

"My staff! Where is my enchanted staff?"

"Be-beep! Let me help look for it, sir," shouted Drill Sergeant, rolling forward. Kaos threw up his hands when he saw the staff with its precious magical crystal lying on the grass in front of Drill Sergeant's bulldozer wheels. "Coming through!"

"Nooooooooo!" Kaos yelled as Drill Sergeant drove straight over the ruby. The metal staff mangled beneath his treads and, with a tinkling crunch and a flash of light, the crystal shattered.

"Oops!" Drill Sergeant grinned. "My bad, sir. My bad!"

There was a fizz of energy, and suddenly Spyro and the Chompy were back to their normal sizes. With a flick of his tail, Spyro batted the Chompy out of the way and turned to see Stealth Elf pop up from the grass.

"Noooooooooooo, you FOOL!" Kaos shrieked, his hands running over his bald head. Spyro was sure that if the Portal Master had hair, he would be pulling it out. "Look what you've done!"

"We've beaten you," giggled Trigger Happy, swinging his pistols around to cover the defeated Portal Master. "That's what we've done. Oh yeah!"

"This was always the plan, wasn't it?" Spyro snarled, stalking forward. "Test your staff out on those other creatures—toads, caterpillars, cockroaches . . . trolls." He glared at Glumshanks, who shrunk back behind his master. "Make people think you were saving them from the monsters, just so you could attack the Archive and blackmail the curator. You thought he would be so blinded by hero worship that he'd just hand over whatever you wanted."

"And he was wrong," shouted Wiggleworth, from his fellow Librarian's hands. "Quite wrong. I'd never give him anything he wanted."

Kaos was surrounded now, cringing on the floor with Glumshanks, while Spyro, Stealth Elf, Trigger Happy, Drill Sergeant, and the remaining Warrior Librarians looked on.

"I suppose you think you've won, dragon breath," he spat, struggling to his feet. "I suppose you think this is all over."

Spyro smiled.

"Looks that way to me."

"Does it now?" Kaos straightened his robes and took a sniff from the orchid in his lapel. When he looked up again, he was smirking. "It's far from over, little dragonfly. If you thought you'd faced your biggest challenge, you were wrong. So, so wrong." The maniacal Portal Master was shouting now, screaming at the top of his maniacal voice. "Hear me. Hear Kaos! This is only the beginning! You are doomed! DOOMED LIKE NEVER BEFORE! DOOOOOOOOMED!" Kaos broke into frenzied laughter and clapped his hands, summoning a Portal. In a flash, he had gone, taking Glumshanks with him.

A tiny scrap of paper floated from where Kaos had stood. Cautiously, Trigger Happy walked over, snatched up the paper and, after glancing at it, held it out for Spyro to read.

"Did I mention that you're doomed? Lots of love, Kaos. x"

Chapter Fourteen

THE BOOK

Spyro waited in the sunshine. All around him, Warrior Librarians bustled here and there. The restoration of the Archive Walls was already underway, and Eon had dispatched every Skylander he could spare to help with the work.

Spyro watched as Trigger Happy, Jet-Vac, and Stealth Elf cleared the rubble, Drill Sergeant and Terrafin dug out new foundations, Prism Break hauled huge piles of bricks back and forth, and Warnado whizzed up gallons of cement, mixed with water from Gill Grunt's water tank. Spyro would join in later, but for now he was

waiting for a very special visitor.

A Portal flashed into existence beside him and Master Eon stepped through the glare. The old man surveyed the damage, but nodded in approval at the sight of his Skylanders working hard to put it right.

"Well done, Spyro," he said gently. "You did well to stop Kaos." He paused before adding, "Again."

Spyro shrugged. "It was a team effort, Master. It's always a team effort."

Eon smiled down at his friend.

"It takes a big dragon to share the glory, Spyro. A big dragon indeed."

Spyro raised his eyebrows.

"Not as big as I was," he said with a grin.

Eon laughed.

"Now, what was it that Wiggleworth wanted to show me?"

The smile faded from Spyro's lips.

"You better come and see for yourself," he said.

The chief curator hadn't been joking. The Archive's vault really was high-security. Spyro and Eon had to walk down seventeen flights of stairs and be let through thirteen heavy metal doors before they reached Wiggleworth, now safely encased in a new suit of armor.

Eon raised a hand in greeting to his old friend. "It's been a long time since I was down here."

"A good many centuries, yes," agreed the curator. "I hardly venture to these depths myself these days, but this is important."

He indicated a large safe set into the far wall.

"Behind this door is one of the most dangerous books in the collection. Some might suggest it's the most dangerous book in the whole of the universe."

Spyro felt his stomach tighten.

"Let me guess—the book Kaos demanded."

The bookworm didn't answer. Instead, his robotic armor clattered and whirred as he walked over to enter a ridiculously long number into a keypad. After what seemed like the hundredth digit, the lock gave a solid clunk and the massive door swung open.

They stepped into the inner chamber. It was completely bare, save for a single book resting on a wooden lectern in the center of the room.

Eon strode over to it. Spyro ran to catch up, coming to a halt beside his master in front of the lectern.

Eon didn't say anything. He just glared down at the cover of the book, a shadow passing over his face.

"Master Eon?" Spyro asked, his voice echoing around the chamber. "What is it?"

There was a long pause before the Portal Master spoke.

"Something I have dreaded for a long time."

Spyro looked up at his master, searching for answers in Eon's worried face.

"This, Spyro, is the legendary Book of Power."

Spyro smiled nervously.

"The Book of Power? That doesn't sound too bad."

Eon gazed down sadly at his favorite Skylander, suddenly looking every inch his impossible age.

"It is a book of prophecy. A book full of the most dreadful predictions."

"Like what?" Spyro asked, a chill running down his tail.

Eon paused, as if he didn't want to say the words out loud.

"Like the fall of the Skylanders, Spyro. And the fall of you."

To be continued in

The Mask of Power:
Gill Grunt and the Curse
of the Fishmaster